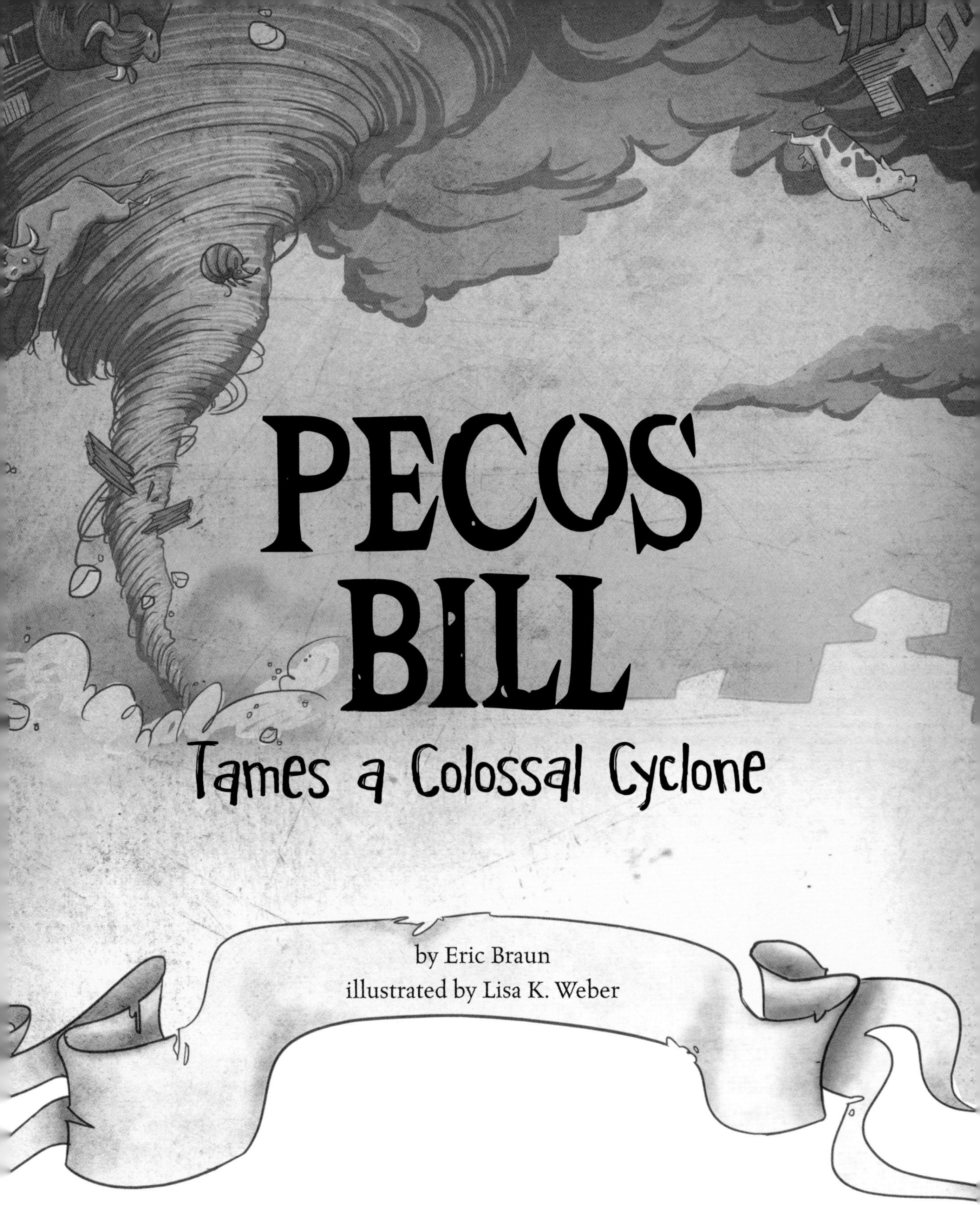

PECOS BILL

Tames a Colossal Cyclone

by Eric Braun

illustrated by Lisa K. Weber

PICTURE WINDOW BOOKS

a capstone imprint

PECOS BILL
An American Cowboy

Long ago in the Old West, cowboys raised cattle on the open land. These cowboys were always on the move. They ate and slept outdoors. They had only each other for family.

Their lives were exciting and free, but hard too. To help forget their troubles, the cowboys told stories around a campfire each night. They told about the amazing adventures of the greatest cowboys. The truth was not important—only great stories were.

Many of these tall tales featured a cowboy who was stronger than any other. He was faster and smarter too. He came to be known as Pecos Bill. According to the stories, Pecos Bill was the greatest cowboy ever. He was an American hero.

The tale of Pecos Bill begins when Bill was just a young'un.
Why, he was no taller than the prairie grass. He lived in Texas
with his ma, pa, and 17 brothers and sisters. To keep track of her
brood, Bill's ma gave all of them a star tattoo on one arm.

Now, Bill's ma and pa were always movin'. They'd pack up
their things—pots, pans, young'uns—and stuff the whole lot in
a covered wagon. Off they'd go, followin' the western-settin' sun.

This here particular summer, they were crossin' the Pecos River into West Texas. Their wagon hit a bump and went ... ka-THUMP.

Next thing you know, Bill went ... a-WHUMP. Li'l feller done flew right off the wagon! Course, with all them noisy young'uns in the wagon, nobody even noticed.

His family gone, Bill lay next to the river, quiet as a sleepin' mouse. Before long an old coyote called Grandy happened along. Ol' Grandy got to thinkin' he should take this human-feller home with him. And so he did.

The coyotes fed Bill coyote milk. It gave him the strength and wisdom of the wild. They taught Bill to run and hunt. Soon enough Bill grew into the strongest boy that ever lived. There was just one catch: Bill thought he was a coyote!

One day when Bill was nearly grown, a feller named Chuck came along. "Hoo-wee," he said. "A person who thinks he's a coyote!"

Chuck watched this coyote-feller run faster than the fastest horse. The feller could split wood with his bare hands! He could talk to varmints in their own languages!

"Hot gravy!" Chuck shouted when he saw Bill's star tattoo. "You're my long-lost brother Bill!"

Chuck introduced Pecos Bill to his cowhand friends. They taught Bill to be a cowboy. And Bill was a right-fast learner. He was as smart as a whip, and as cunning as a coyote.

Soon tales of Pecos Bill's amazing deeds spread far and wide.

Pecos Bill could lasso a herd of cattle in one throw!

Pecos Bill could rope a bald eagle from the sky!

Pecos Bill whipped a 12-foot snake! And he kept it as a pet.

One long, hot summer, the desert got drier than a burnt biscuit.
Every livin' creature was thirsty. Pecos Bill decided to lasso the
Rio Grande River and wet the land. That helped for a while,
but then the land dried up again.

Soon Pecos Bill saw the sky turn green like a big ol' pot of pea soup. In the distance a giant cyclone was suckin' up the earth. This cyclone was monstrous!

"Uh-oh," said Bill. "That's comin' our way!"

The cattle brayed in fear. And the horses were about scared out of their horseshoes!

The cowboys gathered up the livestock and herded them away.

Dirt, rocks, critters, and even houses scattered in the darkenin' sky. An iron teapot got caught up in the cyclone and was spit back down inside out!

Pecos Bill had to think fast. He saddled up his horse and rode right for the cyclone. His lasso whipped into the air. As the cyclone drew near, Bill fired his rope at the top of the funnel. He lassoed that cyclone! But it yanked ol' Bill right off his horse.

Oh, that cyclone was a right handful! It bucked like a wild stallion. But it couldn't throw Bill. It roared into the mountains and ripped them from the earth. It tore across New Mexico, pullin' up trees. The cyclone whipped up its speed, but Bill just smiled.

Next the cyclone raged across Arizona, tearin' a giant hole into the earth. Do you think Pecos Bill let go of that pesky thing?

You can bet your breakfast he did not! He held on tighter than a rattlesnake holds its rattle.

Well, that was enough for the cyclone. Worn out and broken down, it slowed its spinnin'. Then it poured rain into the hole it had carved. The huge rush of water formed the Colorado River.

That hole later became the Grand Canyon.

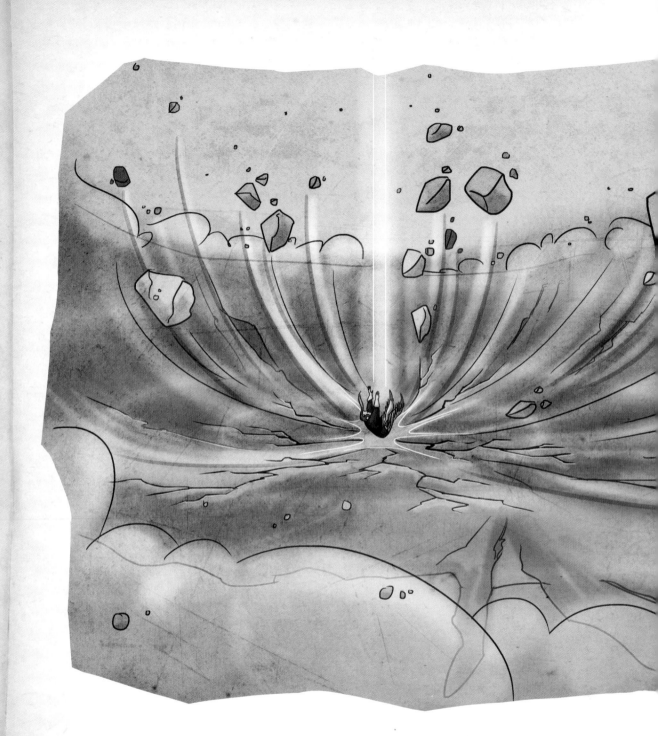

As the cyclone petered out, Pecos Bill saw that he was goin' to fall. So, he leapt as high as he could. When he landed in the desert, his body went ... ka-THUMP. His crash made a huge hole.

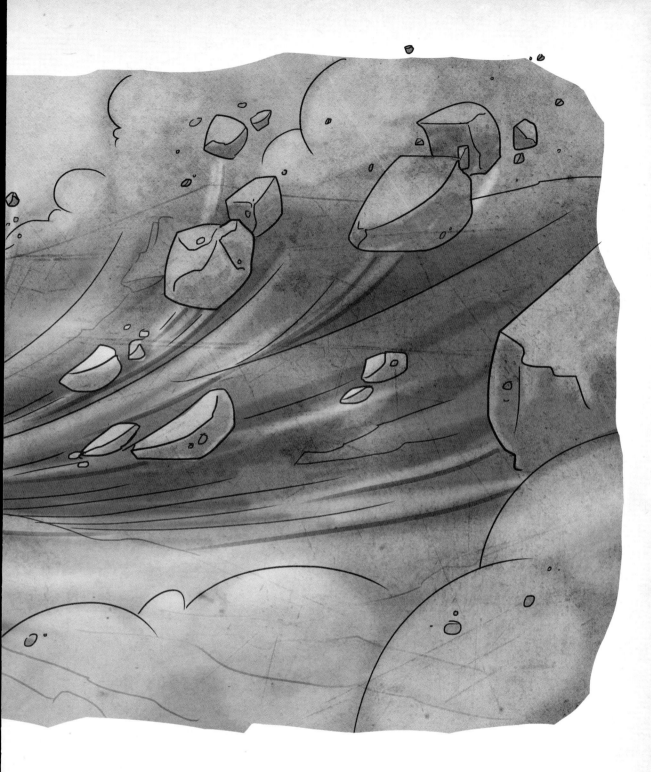

Today the hole is known as Death Valley.

When Bill awoke the coyotes had saved him, just as they had when he was a young'un. Them rascals licked his wounds and kept him safe. They fed him coyote milk.

When he was ready, they helped him find his men.

"Hot gravy!" said Chuck when Pecos Bill came home.
"Am I glad to see you again!"

Bill roped a steer and said, "Brother, my adventures are
just beginning."

The first stories about a cowboy hero were told during the 1800s. Cowboys sat by their campfires and spun tall tales. The hero had different names, but in 1923, a soldier, adventurer, and writer named Edward S. "Tex" O'Reilly wrote down many of the stories. He called the cowboy Pecos Bill and published the stories in an article called "The Saga of Pecos Bill." It was the first written collection of Pecos Bill stories. In them, Bill was not always a good guy. He robbed trains and stole horses. And he rode the cyclone for fun rather than to save his friends.

A few years later, a writer named Mody Boatright wrote a longer article, adding to the stories. Finally in 1937, a whole book was published about Pecos Bill. This brought the legend of Pecos Bill to its biggest audience yet. The author, James Cloyd Bowman, added to the stories even more. He painted Bill as a good-hearted hero, instead of a bad guy.

In 1948 Disney released a movie called *Melody Time*. It told seven "classic" stories, including the saga of Pecos Bill. In this movie, as in the stories written before, Pecos Bill met a woman named Slue-Foot Sue, who became his wife. Sue was a powerful hero like Bill. She rode down the Rio Grande on the back of a catfish.

Disney made another movie about Pecos Bill in 1995 called *Tall Tale: The Unbelievable Adventures of Pecos Bill*.

Learn More About Folktales

Although there are many different American folktales, each story contains similar pieces. Take a look at what usually makes up an American folktale:

hero—the main character of an American folktale is most often a hero with exaggerated abilities, or abilities that seem greater than they actually are

humor—most early American folktales are funny; the exaggerated characters and situations add to the humor

hyperbole—exaggeration; used in folktales to make the characters seem larger than life, almost magical

quest—a challenge; most early American folktales include a challenge that the main character faces; the challenge may include defeating a villain

slang—words and phrases that are more often used in speech, and are usually used by a certain group of people; common cowboy slang consisted of words and sayings such as "There's no use beatin' the devil around the stump," which meant there's no use avoiding a difficult task

Critical Thinking Using the Common Core

1. American folktales often include a quest or challenge. What was Pecos Bill's big challenge in this story? (Key Ideas and Details)

2. If you could retell a story from your past, what details would you include and why? Which common folktale elements could you use to make the story even more exciting? (Integration of Knowledge and Ideas)

Glossary

brood—children

cattle—cows, bulls, and steers raised for food

cowboy—a man who looks after cattle

coyote—an animal similar to a wolf

cunning—intelligent; sneaky or clever at tricking people

cyclone—a storm with strong winds that blow around a center; also called a tornado

folktale—a traditional, timeless tale people enjoy telling

legend—a story handed down from earlier times; legends may be based on facts, but they are not entirely true

varmint—a wild animal

wisdom—knowledge, experience, and good judgement

Read More

Blair, Eric. *Pecos Bill: A Retelling by Eric Blair*. My First Classic Story. Mankato, Minn.: Picture Window Books, 2011.

Strauss, Kevin. *Pecos Bill Invents the Ten-Gallon Hat*. Gretna, La.: Pelican Publishing, 2012.

Tulien, Sean, retold by. *Pecos Bill, Colossal Cowboy*. Graphic Spin. Mankato, Minn.: Stone Arch Books, 2010.

Editor's Note: This story is adapted from a story in *Pecos Bill: The Greatest Cowboy of All Time*, by James Cloyd Bowman.

Thanks to our advisers for their expertise, research, and advice:

Elizabeth Tucker Gould, Professor of English
Binghamton University

Terry Flaherty, PhD, Professor of English
Minnesota State University, Mankato

Editor: Shelly Lyons
Designer: Tracy Davies McCabe
Art Director: Nathan Gassman
Production Specialist: Jennifer Walker
The illustrations in this book were created digitally.

Design element: Shutterstock: 06photo

Picture Window Books are published by Capstone,
1710 Roe Crest Drive, North Mankato, Minnesota 56003

Library of Congress Cataloging-in-Publication Data
Braun, Eric, 1971–
Pecos Bill tames a colossal cyclone / by Eric Braun.
pages cm.—(Picture window books. American folk legends)
Adapted from a story in Pecos Bill, the greatest cowboy of all time, by James Cloyd Bowman.
Summary: Super-cowboy Pecos Bill leaps onto the back of a monstrous cyclone and rides it like a bucking bronco, creating, in the process, the Colorado River, the Grand Canyon, and Death Valley.
Includes bibliographical references.
ISBN 978-1-4795-5429-4 (library binding)
ISBN 978-1-4795-5446-1 (paperback)
ISBN 978-1-4795-5454-6 (eBook PDF)
1. Pecos Bill (Legendary character)—Legends. [1. Pecos Bill (Legendary character)—Legends. 2. Folklore—United States. 3. Tall tales.] I. Bowman, James Cloyd, 1880–1961. Pecos Bill, the greatest cowboy of all time. II. Title.
PZ8.1.B73633Pe 2015
398.2—dc23 [E]   2014001490

Printed in the United States of America
in North Mankato, MN.
032014   008087CGF14

Internet Sites

FactHound offers a safe, fun way to find Internet sites related to this book. All of the sites on FactHound have been researched by our staff.

Here's all you do:

Visit *www.facthound.com*

Type in this code: 9781479554294

Super-cool stuff! Check out projects, games and lots more at **www.capstonekids.com**

Look for all the books in the series:

Davy Crockett and the Great Mississippi Snag
John Henry vs. the Mighty Steam Drill
Johnny Appleseed Plants Trees Across the Land
Pecos Bill Tames a Colossal Cyclone

PATRICIA BRIGGS

MERCY THOMPSON

homecoming

written by
patricia briggs
and **david lawrence**

painted artwork by
francis tsai and amelia woo

lettering by
bill tortolini

edited by
david lawrence
and **rich young**

ballantine books · new york

PATRICIA BRIGGS

MERCY THOMPSON

homecoming

thanks to thematic consultants
linda campbell, debbie lentz, and jenifer phillips linthwaite

Published in the United States by Del Rey,
an imprint of The Random House Publishing Group,
a division of Random House, Inc., New York.

DEL REY is a registered trademark and the Del Rey colophon
is a trademark of Random House, Inc.

ISBN 978-0-345-50988-8

Printed in the United States of America on acid-free paper

www.delreybooks.com
www.dabelbrothers.com

9 8 7 6 5 4 3 2 1

First Edition

Designed by Bill Tortolini

publisher
ERNST DABEL

v.p. business operations
LES DABEL

business development
RICH YOUNG

project manager
DEREK RUIZ

consulting editor
DAVID LAWRENCE

special projects
DAVID DABEL

graphic design
LITHIUM PRO

CHAPTER ONE
WOLF AT THE DOOR!

cover artwork by
brett booth
and **georgi valchev**

CHAPTER TWO
HUNGRY LIKE THE WOLF!

I'M HERE, AREN'T I?

AND YOU'RE CERTAINLY MORE [PLE]ASANT THAN YOUR [F]RIEND WAS LAST NIGHT.

MARKUS? IT WAS A *MISTAKE* TO SEND HIM TO THE GARAGE. HE IS YOUNG, DRUNK WITH HIS POWER AND HAS A PARTICULAR *DISLIKE* FOR THE FAE.

I THOUGHT THERE MIGHT BE *TROUBLE*.

AND OUT OF THE *GOODNESS* OF YOUR HEART YOU THOUGHT YOU'D PREVENT IT?

IT IS *POSSIBLE*, YOU KNOW.

HONESTLY, THE *SEETHE* DOES NOT NEED AN ENEMY AS *POWERFUL* AS SIEBOLD ADELBERTSMITER--

PARTICULARLY IN HIS *CURRENT* STATE OF MIND.

"HAVE YOU MET YOUR EMPLOYER?"

"THAT'S *HIM*?"

"HE HASN'T BEEN IN HIS RIGHT MIND SINCE HIS WIFE DIED. HE'S A DANGER TO HIMSELF AND *OTHERS*."

"HUMAN AND IMMORTAL FAE SHOULD *NOT* MATE."

CHAPTER THREE
CRY WOLF!

NORMALLY, WEREWOLVES *SHUN HUMANS.*

I THOUGHT THE NEXT APARTMENT, OVER A GARAGE, MIGHT WORK.

IT WOULD CERTAINLY OFFER MORE **PRIVACY**--

BUT THAT WAS THE **ONLY** GOOD THING I COULD SAY ABOUT IT.

PLUS, IT WAS OWNED BY A JUDGMENTAL OLD **HAG**--

WHO GOT ONE LOOK AT MY **TATOO** AND DECIDED I WAS THE DRUG-DEALING WHORE OF BABYLON.

I HAD A GOOD **LAUGH** AT HER EXPENSE--

BUT IT DIDN'T GET ME ANY CLOSER TO FINDING A **HOME**.

GGRRRAAGHHRR

CHAPTER FOUR
BLOOD MOON

SO WHY DID I HAVE MY FOSTER FATHER'S GUNS OUT?

HAUPTMAN COULD TAKE CARE OF HIMSELF, **OR** THE MARROK WOULDN'T HAVE SENT HIM.

BESIDES, I **WASN'T** A WEREWOLF, AND CLEARLY THEY DIDN'T WANT ME AROUND--

ANY MORE THAN BRAN HAD, WHEN I WAS SIXTEEN AND HE SENT ME **AWAY**...

KNOCK KNOCK

IT'S A LITTLE *LATE* FOR VISITORS. I HAVE TO WORK IN THE MORNING.

THIS WON'T TAKE *LONG*.

I HAD A CHAT WITH OUR *FAVORITE* VAMPIRE.

WE HAVE A FAVORITE VAMPIRE?

STEFAN SAYS THAT YOU *STOOD UP* FOR MY SON.

TAD'S COOL.

CAN'T HELP *WHO* HE'S RELATED TO.

SO--

EVENTUALLY, A FEW *OTHERS* ARRIVED, CLIMBING THE HILL AND FINDING HIDING PLACES OF THEIR OWN.

THEY WERE WOLVES. MUST HAVE BEEN ADAM'S. THEY WERE WELL BEHAVED AND THEIR SCENT GAVE NO HINT THEY'D BEEN FEASTING ON *HUMANS.*

NIGHT WAS FALLING AS THE REST ARRIVED. ADAM'S PACK ALMOST *SPARKLED* WITH SPIT-SHINE AND DISCIPLINE. ORSON'S--

WELL, THEY LOOKED LIKED LIKED THE UNRULY *ROGUES* THEY WERE.

YOUR *CALL*, PARK. HUMAN--

OR *WOLF?*

WOLF.

IT SUITS MY *TRUE* NATURE.

BEFORE WE *BEGIN*-- THE BOY *AND* MY WOLF.

HOME SWEET HOME-- AT LAST.

THE END.

art gallery

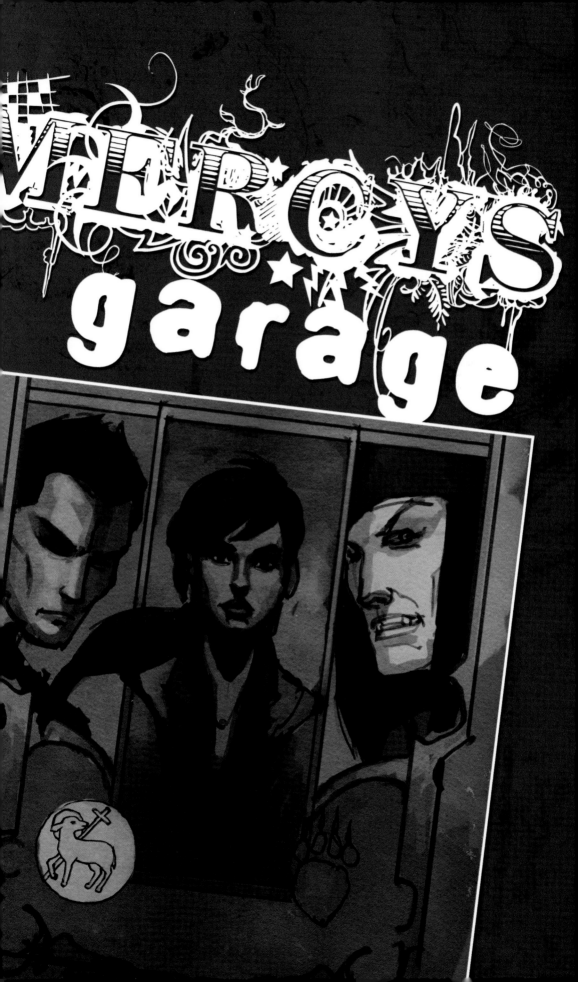

MERCY

TAD

ADAM

DARRYL

BRAN

STEFAN

an interview with
patricia briggs

by david lawrence

Owing to the vagaries of comic book scheduling, a mid-stream switch of artists, and other events too sundry to mention, it's been just about a year since Patty and I began our collaboration on this project.

We've exchanged probably hundreds of e-mails, written and revised dozens and dozens of pages, talked on the phone once or twice, and in my case, at least, added considerably to my growing collection of gray hair.

But honestly, it's been a blast. From the very opening sequence of the very first issue to the last scene of the last, I've grown very fond of Mercy and her friends. Particularly Zee, which I suspect owes something to our mutual devotion to the Pittsburgh Steelers.

As we wind up, it seems like the perfect time to sit back and reflect on what we've done, and what the future might hold in comics for Mercy Thompson.

How did MERCY THOMPSON: HOMECOMING come to be? Did the idea of a graphic novel originate with you, or your publisher, or did the Dabels initiate it?

The Dabel Brothers originally asked if I had a short story, or wanted to tell a shorter story to start off the comic editions of the Mercy Thompson books. As it happens, I had a whole bunch of material I'd written before I wrote IRON KISSED—about how Mercy and her mentor, Zee, had met. It struck me that, combined with the story of how Adam Hauptman and his band of Merry Wolves had ended up in the Tri Cities, it might make a dandy Origin Story—the kind of story that comics do so well.

Were you familiar at all with Dabel Brothers publishing previously? If you were, what projects had you seen or heard about?

I knew who the Dabel Brothers were, having seen the work they were doing with Laurell K. Hamilton's Anita Blake books. I was then, and still am, incredibly impressed with their work. Not only the quality, but the ability to put just the right artist with the right works of fiction, so that fans of the novels also love the artwork.

Was the story itself something you'd had in mind as Mercy's back story for a while, or something cooked up entirely from scratch as you began work on the series?

I had bits and scraps of stories that I shook up and put together for the comics.

Some of the writers I've worked with, like Jim Butcher for example, are pretty well versed in comics. Did you have any background in the medium? Did you read any comics as a kid, have any favorite characters? Any writers or artists in the medium you were familiar with?

I read comics a lot as a child, from, say, the early seventies up through about 1980 or so. I liked the X-Men and Spider-Man, but most of the ones I really loved were the lesser-known series. Stuff like Claws of the Cat, Shanna the She-Devil, Ka-Zar, the Inhumans, and the sadly anonymous Black Orchid, who is remembered by precious few. And of course, Werewolf by Night.

Jack Kirby I knew. Who could not? My favorite of his works was a DC comic, The Demon. But for the most part I hadn't gotten to the point of recognizing authors and artists by the time I set comics aside for books.

What did you think the first time you sat down and tried to write a comic book script?

The initial layout isn't hard. And really, although the kinds of stories that work best visually and the kinds that work best in a book are different, storytelling works the same either way. Some things are easier; setting, for instance. Some things are tougher; plotting without words and putting my hands up and saying, "The artist can convey this better than I can."

The most miserable thing is the revisions. Add another panel for clarity or effect, and you throw the visual rhythm completely off. It took me a long time and I was very happy to turn it over to you, who can work your magic much faster and more skillfully than I could!

It's a pretty big change for a novelist, I'd think, suddenly having a bunch of collaborators to work with. You're used to being pretty solitary in your work. What was it like to suddenly have all these other people involved? Was there anything in particular you liked and disliked about it?

First of all, I can't tell you how incredibly cool it is to see your fictional characters appear visually. I've seen it before, of course, with the book covers, but only with the primary characters. Seeing some of these people for the first time was . . . wow! I thought, "So that's what Darryl looks like. That's perfect!"

It is also great to share responsibility. If something doesn't quite work well I have a number of other people who can catch it. If it does work, I have people to celebrate with. Happily, because it is in a medium I'm no expert in, I found that my control-freak issues weren't as prevalent as I feared.

What was the biggest surprise for you?

I think it is how active a role I've gotten to take in bringing Mercy and her world into the realm of comic books.

Are there any sequences you particularly liked in the series or anything that didn't work that you'd like to have back and try again?

I particularly like the way Zee comes out in HOME-COMING. The artists caught him just right. I also like the flow of the story in the second comic: all your idea, I might add.

One sequence I have to ask you about. I noticed on your message board the long sequence at the beginning of the first chapter, with naked Mercy fighting the wolf pack, seemed to create quite a stir. And I know that I really kind of took your original sequence there and put it on steroids. What was your reaction when you saw it?

I liked it quite a bit. One of the decisions I made, to keep the stories feeling real, was to keep clothes as an obstacle for changing shape. The comic sequence makes it quite clear just how big of an obstacle it is!

As things turned out, we had two different artists for the series, Francis Tsai and Amelia Woo. Both did great work. I'm wondering how they compare in your mind. What things did you like better about Francis's work and what did you like better about Amelia's?

Francis has a clear style that reminds me a bit of Jack Kirby's work, not so much in execution, but in distinctiveness. Amelia has a softer style and her women are a little less sexualized. Both of them are terrific.

It's got to be a tough experience on some level for you, allowing another writer to work with your characters. And you've admitted you're a control freak. How hard was it for you to let me into your sandbox?

It helps that you are terrific. Makes it less of a struggle. It also helps that writing a comic book is a freaking lot of work and you are a lot faster at it than I would be. It was incredibly helpful to be able to send you part of a short story and have you return with a script.

What do you see now as the biggest differences between telling a story in prose and telling it with pictures?

In a primarily visual media, we had to cut down the internal dialogue and keep the conversation short and to the point. A book allows a lot more internal dialogue. Of course, physical descriptions are a lot easier in comics.

With HOMECOMING behind us, Dabel Brothers will be adapting some of your novels. Are you planning on doing any more original-for-comics stories with your characters, or just adaptations for the time being?

For right now, I'm still behind the eight ball with my books. I'm not opposed to doing some direct-to-comic stories, but I imagine that will be a year or more down the line.

Now you've been wonderful to work with, and very gracious, but I've got to ask: Was there ever a time when you just wanted to kill me?

Kiss you, when you took ten pages of rough draft and turned it into a pretty terrific story, but never kill you. Especially after you listened to me about the scene where Mercy and Stefan are dropping off Zee and noticed you missed the perfect response—and you fixed it. No, you are very easy to work with.

Do you have any words of advice for another novelist who might be out there, considering following in your footsteps and trying their hand at comics?

Find someone who knows what they're doing and listen to them!